PALISADES FREE LIBRARY

3 2829 00025 3835

W9-DFN-175

I Was A Second Grade Werewolf

by Daniel Pinkwater

Puffin Unicorn

Copyright © 1983 by Daniel Pinkwater
All rights reserved.

Unicorn is a registered trademark of E. P. Dutton.

Library of Congress number 82-17715
ISBN 0-525-44194-8

Published in the United States by
Dutton Children's Books
A Division of Penguin USA
375 Hudson Street
New York, NY 10014

Published simultaneously in Canada by
Fitzhenry & Whiteside Limited, Toronto

Editor: Ann Durell   Designer: Riki Levinson
Printed in Hong Kong by South China Printing Co.
First Unicorn Edition 1985   COBE
10   9   8

to Ann Durell—
who knows a werewolf
when she sees one

When I woke up in the morning, I saw that
the backs of my hands were covered with hair.
I looked in the mirror.

My face was all hairy too. My nose was
different. I had long sharp teeth.
I knew what had happened.
"I have turned into a werewolf," I said.
"Neat!"

My mother called me to breakfast. I wonder
what they'll say when they see I'm a werewolf,
I thought.

They didn't say anything. Breakfast was the same as it was every day.

I ate cereal, orange juice, milk, and my little brother's plastic cup with a picture of a spaceman on it. Nobody said anything special.

"Lawrence, stop snarling at your sister," my mother said.

I walked to school with the usual bunch of kids. I thought someone would say something. I thought someone would notice that I was a werewolf.

Nobody did.

I walked part of the way to school, and ran part of the way on all fours. I got there ahead of my friends.

My teacher is Mrs. Packman. I was sure she would say something. She's very strict.

Mrs. Packman didn't say anything. I sit in the back of the room. Maybe she didn't see me.

I bit the shoulder of the girl who sits in front of me, Loretta Parsnip.

"Mrs. Packman! Lawrence Talbot bit me!" Loretta Parsnip said.

Now she'll notice, I thought. I'll bet she screams.

"Lawrence, behave yourself," Mrs. Packman said. That's all.

I was getting mad. Why was everyone pretending not to notice that I had changed into a werewolf? I ate a pencil.

Mrs. Packman read a story to the class. It was about a fuzzy blue bunny. She held up the book to show us the pictures.

"Who is growling?" Mrs. Packman asked. "Lawrence Talbot, are you growling? Stop that noise!"

I ate lunch with my best friend, James Ballpoint. I ate a cardboard milk carton and a Twinkie with the cellophane on it. "That's neat," James said.

"Do you see anything different
about me?" I asked.
"Nope," James said.
"I'm a werewolf," I said.

"Great!" James said. "I'm a werewolf too."

"No you're not," I said.

"Why not? Why can't I be a werewolf too?"

"Because I'm a real werewolf. It's not some stupid game."

"I think you're stupid,"
James said, and walked away.
He gets mad like that.

I was standing by the iron fence around
the school.

I bent some of the bars.

I walked home by myself after school.

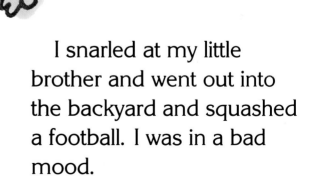

I snarled at my little brother and went out into the backyard and squashed a football. I was in a bad mood.

I didn't bother to say anything to my family at supper. I just lapped up my food.

That night I climbed out through the window
and ran through the streets on all fours.

I howled at the moon. I had a pretty
good time.

The next morning, I looked in the mirror and noticed that I was not a werewolf.

My mother called me to breakfast.

"Did you have a good night, Lawrence?" she asked.

"Yes," I said.

Everything was back to normal. Nobody had noticed anything.

The next time I turn into a werewolf, it's going to be different.